boucaud in the story:
2013−2017

boucaud in the story:
2013−2017

s. i. boucaud

IGUANA

Copyright © 2017 s. i. boucaud
Published by Iguana Books
720 Bathurst Street, Suite 303
Toronto, Ontario, Canada
M5S 2R4

All rights reserved. No part of this publication may be reproduced, stored in a retrieval system or transmitted, in any form or by any means, electronic, mechanical, recording or otherwise (except brief passages for purposes of review) without the prior permission of the author or a licence from The Canadian Copyright Licensing Agency (Access Copyright). For an Access Copyright licence, visit www.accesscopyright.ca or call toll free to 1-800-893-5777.

Publisher: Mary Ann J. Blair
Editor: Jen R. Albert
Front cover image: iStock
Cover design: Jessica Albert

ISBN 978-1-77180-236-9 (paperback)
ISBN 978-1-77180-238-3 (EPUB)
ISBN 978-1-77180-237-6 (Kindle)

This book contains stories and poems I authored between 2013 and 2017. There will be no further updates to them. It is time to lay them to rest, to be woken up by others.

This book does not contain artwork. To obtain the artwork I created for some of the stories, please go to www.amazon.ca and search for ISBN 978-0-9940665-2-7.

This is an original print edition of *boucaud in the story: 2013–2017*.

I would like to dedicate this book to all the storytellers and listeners who have encouraged my telling and writing.

Contents

A Very Shy Boy	1
An Unwelcomed Friend of Yours	4
The Loving	6
Jackal	8
Taking This Time to Tell You (poem)	13
Fish with Bellies	15
Her Cocoon Fat (poem)	16
Them Lovely Hips	17
The Watch Observer and His Beloved	19
Selection (poem)	23
The Distraction	24
A New Place	27
The Witness Giver	29
I Ain't Goin' Down No Rabbit Hole	32
The Journey of Deleted Pathways	36
The White Brown Girl	39
Mama	39
After Mama Died	41
The Shifting	42
The Reconciling	43
The Restitution	45
Forgiveness	47
Whisper Spirits (poem)	49

Unknown to Known	52
The Firing	54
Suspenders and a Belt	56
An Agreed Upon Time	60
Done with You	61
In the Passing (poem)	64
The Man with the Hound Dog Face	66
Once Again, Sound Rescues Truth	69
Jeep Drivers	71
Behind the Soft Black Eyes	72
Before the Shared Path (poem)	75
Daya	77
The Weight Loser	79
Driving on the Rims of God's Eyelashes (poem)	81
The Young Little Dog	82
Maler and the Troll	84
The Eagle Cried	87
She Led (poem)	89
Who Is the Host?	91
Remember	99
In the Wound, Wounding	100
Priya	104

A Very Shy Boy

All three, (grandmother, mother, and daughter) sat there. Their legs were spread wide. The difference for him was the visibility. The grandmother's dress covered her ankles, the mother's dress covered her knees, and the daughter's dress covered the mid part of her thigh. She was the one being viewed and he knew she was oblivious to the effect the view was having on him.

He was so grateful that the covering he wore over both thighs was made of a fairly thick cloth. His desire was just touching the inside of the cloth that hung over his lap. When she looked in his direction, his eyes darted away from her. The fear of his body betraying his desire for her necessitated him — for the rest of the viewing — to look, in a fixed manner, in the direction of the floor. She took this as a sign of rejection.

After the viewing was over, she went into her room and cried. Her immediate and extended family soothed her by telling her that he was a shy boy. A very shy boy. In the olden days — according to her grandmother —

people did not meet beforehand. They continually told her that he had not rejected her.

It was her cousin who had spoken to her about him. He was, she said, a man who liked to grow plants. They grew very healthy under his care. He also, she said, liked to help animals who were sick. Often, he healed the animals. The response of the animals and plants under his care informed her that was a good man. She — based on the reports — decided to marry him. Therefore, his behaviour — which she thought was rejection — disappointed her greatly.

Having no knowledge of his or any other man's desire, you can imagine her surprise and delight when the dowry was accepted by his family.

After the sixth child, she was lying in bed with him beside her. The room was dark, and all she heard was his awake breathing. Clearing her throat — something he noticed she did when she was nervous — she asked him how it was that by the afternoon on the day he first saw her he accepted the dowry. He was surprised by the question and remained quiet for a little while. When he spoke, he asked her how it was that she could ask him such a question when she knew how much he loved her. She told him that she knew of his love but that he had looked away from her as though he had rejected her, and yet on the same day his family accepted the dowry. She wanted to know, she told him, what happened.

His heart warmed his whole body. Turning towards her in the dark he slowly placed his head on her breasts and sighed. He knew in his soul that she had no idea how close he had come to embarrassing himself and being perceived as disrespectful to her mother and grandmother. Deciding not to tell her, he told her that he was hers forever and had been since time began. He then fell asleep.

After they had their fifteenth grandchild, she was no wiser to knowing why — so many years ago on the viewing day — he looked away. Holding her grandchild she recalled — so many years ago — his last breath. She recalled asking her question again, but it had remained unanswered. All he did was smile lovingly at her and then pass to the other world.

Rocking her grandchild back and forth she thought to herself, "They must have been right. He must have been a very shy boy during the day of the viewing. A very shy boy."

An Unwelcomed Friend of Yours

I wondered how it would end. You were too civilized to stand your ground and raise your fist; far too refined for such a gesture. Defiance, any gesture of defiance, was definitely beyond you.

I don't really recall when you left. Isn't that the saddest part of all? It would have been better — I think — if there were some defining line. An end point. Instead, one day I looked up, and you were nowhere to be found.

Depression is such an ugly illness. I stood beside it amazed at the way it twirled and whirled around you while at the same time, inch by inch, burrowing itself deep down into your soul.

I want you to know that your depression never let me down. From day one it told me that jobs that you did around the house would at best be half-done. It told me that you would always gravitate to some outside chaos that you hoped would provide you a spark to inflame your energy.

At least now that you are gone there is no pretension that I can rely on someone. Don't get me wrong, I have no grudge against you. To you I send a blessing, plenty of blessings. But I do want you to know that if you decide to return, I have made a decision about your depression friend. I know you two are very close, but I no longer want your friend in my home. It is an unwelcomed friend.

The Loving

It was well-known that they always associated with each other.

The end of their day began after the children were in their beds. Sometimes hands were held in exhausted silence. Other times, concerns were uttered at such blinding speeds that the content was lost. All that was left were various emotions, emotions that hung around like clouds of smoke after a fire.

As the children grew, there were spaces for conversations that were not run-on sentences. Pauses between sentences were established and welcomed by the listener.

When the children left, the end of the day was marked by a cuddle; bodies got reacquainted with each other and snores could be heard arising from deep inside of their bodies.

They arrived together at a pension. The constricted days of the past were gone.

They found themselves thrilled with the new adventures they brought into each of their days.

Conversations echoed smiles of contentment. Pauses between sentences remained. Handholding and cuddling occurred with greater frequency.

The funeral home made an extra-large casket. Everyone was pleased. It seemed only fitting that they be buried together.

Jackal

Picking up the mirror, she lovingly looked at her smooth face. She had seen him put out his Sunday clothes. All of them did this before they entered her.

He was the worst one. This one always left those long fine crisscross beard scratch lines on her face.

"I getting ready," he called out to her.

Looking deeply and lovingly at her face in the mirror, she told Her that all would be right. She started to lullaby Her to sleep. Just as she was tucking Her far away from him, the door banged.

"We gots a Jackal," shouted a voice she did not recognize. "Up in the tree."

She grabbed her axe — the one with the long handle and razor sharp blades on both sides of its head — from underneath her bed. Axe in one hand and skinning knife in the other, she ran in the direction of her brothers. There was the Jackal in the tree.

"Jackal, you better come down," said one of her brothers.

The other brother raised his rifle and aimed it in the direction of the tree. Standing on the raised ground, she was behind all four of them.

In hope of catching the attention of the Jackal, she raised the axe and moved it back and forth above her head. The Jackal saw her. She took her left middle finger and moved it slowly across her throat.

"Jackal," said her brother, "if yous don't come down I'm gonna have my brother here shoot them legs off yous. Now you come down."

She and the Jackal's eyes connected. The Jackal raised both of his hands and wrapped them around the branch. Quickly looking at her, he moved his head in a downward motion. She knew then that she had gotten his permission. Just like all of those times in the past, she knew what to do.

The gun fired, and she, axe raised in the air, ran towards the body that was falling.

The dogs growled. They showed their teeth.

"You wants some of that Jackal, don't you boys? Some good old Jackal meat. Well, yous just go down on him and gets yous full of him," said the brother laughing.

He then released the dogs.

She got to the Jackal before the dogs did. His eyes smiled at her as he arched his neck up towards her axe. It slid through the neck of the Jackal like a hot knife sliding through butter.

Grabbing the Jackal's hair, she threw the head in the direction of the dogs. Then with the skinning knife, she cut out chunks of the body and threw the pieces to the dogs. They never got near to the Jackal's bones.

It was in the darkness of the night she usually gave the Jackals' bones a decent burial.

After the skinning was all over, he called out to her.

"Go hose yourself down. I getten ready," he said. She did so.

When she returned to the room she picked up the mirror and softly sang Her a lullaby. She began to tuck Her far, far away from him as he scrubbed himself down.

They — all four brothers — scrubbed themselves down before they put on their Sunday suit. "Likes that would make it all proper to enter their sister," she laughed and winked at Her in the mirror.

"Off yous go," she said to Her, "that's it. Off yous go," and she placed the mirror face down on her dresser.

After it was over, she took the mirror and whispered to Her. "It's okay. You can come back now."

Looking for Her but not seeing Her she said, "He's finished. It's okay, come back. You listening to me?"

It seemed like hours had passed since she had last seen Her. A feeling — which she could not identify — crept into her body. She tried to sleep but could not sleep. The unidentified feeling, she realized was loneliness.

Trying to feel good, she thought of the Jackal. She recalled the smiling eyes of the Jackal. She felt his gratitude about being killed quickly before the dogs got to him. She felt his appreciation for keeping the dogs away from his bones. The Jackals believed that unmarked bones allowed the dead to go to heaven; marked bones meant they would remain in hell (which for them was this earth).

Then her mind wandered over to the smiling eyes of all the Jackals she had axed.

She reached under the bed and took the axe in bed with her. Neither the axe nor the memories helped her with the loneliness. It consumed her like a cancer.

After burying the bones alongside the other bones of the Jackals she had killed, she returned to her bedroom.

Moonbeams started to flood the room. Unable to sleep, she left the room. Walking past her brothers, she found herself opening the door that led to the outside of the house.

The dogs looked at her. She looked at the dogs. Neither made a sound as she untied them. Like shadows, they followed her into the house and then sat in a line in front of her sleeping brothers.

She reached for the newly sharpened skinning knife that hung on the kitchen wall and proceeded to slit each one of her brothers' throats. The sharpened skinning knife silently slid through skin and bones, like a hot knife sliding through butter.

The dogs advanced after she left the bodies. In pack-like formation they feasted on the bodies.

Locating the mirror, she looked into it and frantically searched for Her. She pleaded to Her to return.

"Tis all taken care of," she said. "Listen to me now. Tis all taken care of. You wants me to sing to yous like our Mama did? Is that whats you wants? Yous can't stay back there forever. Yous listening? I wants you back. Come on back now. Theys not here."

Suddenly — in the depth of one eye — she saw Her.

"Ah, there's you is," she sighed.

At the sight of Her, the lonely feeling disappeared.

"Now don't you mind them scratches. When these gone there is no more coming back. He and alls them, theys gone now. Yous don't got to hide away no more. No more. Yous hear me now. No more."

She smiled at the dogs feasting on her brothers. Then taking the sharpened axe in one hand and the clean newly sharpened skinning knife in the other hand, she left the house. The dogs followed her one by one.

Taking This Time to Tell You

Did I tell you how much
I love you today?

Did I tell you how much
I love
your
balding head
which captures the sun,
your gray mustache
with food particles all over it?

Did I tell you how much
I love you today?

Did I tell how much
I love
the
roar of your laughter
which captures our joy,

the twinkling of your eyes
which are surrounded by our laugh lines?

Did I tell you how much
I love you today?

Did I tell you how much
I love
your
shirt slightly hanging
over your unpressed pants,
the ups and downs of passed years
the mileage we have travelled?

Did I tell you how much I love you today?
If not, then I am taking this pen to paper and telling you now.

Fish with Bellies

Fish with bellies floated on the surface of the river and washed onto the shore. My teenage heart felt heavy.

Paddles stroked the water creating small ripples. The fish, with their bellies visible for all to see, surrounded the paddle boat. Laughter filled the air. Those in the boat were oblivious to the fish. I kept looking, from the shore, to find some form of objection to what was visibly floating around the paddle boat. There was none.

Time marched on. Relationships formed, dissolved, and formed again. A child was born and grown. I then returned to that shore.

My fifty-year-old heart felt happy.

"What's the fishing like?" I called out. A thumbs up gesture and a big smile spread across the face of the fisher.

Scanning the river I walked in the place where the water stroked the shore. The happiness I felt soared. There were no dead fish washed onto the shore or any floating fish bellies in the water. How lovely.

Her Cocoon Fat

She snuggled into her fat
ready for the winter
Her hands rested
on top of her stomach
as the upper part of her arms
warmed the side of her body
Cocooned

Them Lovely Hips

Oh my, what lovely hips that one has. No, no, no … no babies coming from them hips. Could be some coming from that one; not sure. Think I'll pass on them hips.

All that fuss with Children's Aid. Damn Children's Aid, gots me out here again lookin'. Still, she gave me all girls, just like I wanted. Gots no use for boys. Only good for the dogs.

Good thing that one ended up in the psych ward. Great country with all them lawyers. Still she was trouble. Rest just fell in line but not she. She was good when young though. Real good.

They was good times those days. Had all those girls trained just right. Stupid teachers phoning the Children's Aid just cause she cut herself all up. Stupid teachers and that psych ward. Listening to all her whining and carrying on. Ruined it, just ruined it all. Damn teachers, damn Children's Aid, damn psych ward; they gots me out here again, lookin' again. They should of left everything all right.

What's that over there. Oh, I think I gots the right one. Yup, those hips will do just fine. Thinks I will take this one to the woods. No psych ward, no Children's Aid, no teachers in them woods. There'll be lots of babies coming down the shoot with them hips. Gots no use for boys. The river will take care of them.

The Watch Observer and His Beloved

He looked at the paper; his eyes did not move. After a period of time, his fingers touched his watch. Nodding his head, he proceeded to look and turn the newspaper. Eyes not moving, his mouth made movements as though uttering words. I glanced at him over my cup of coffee. His smile was radiant.

Initially, it was not clear to me what caught my attention. Was it the way his hair was combed back from his face? Was it the straightness of his back or the long thick fingers that cupped the newspaper? After observing him for a period, I decided that it was none of the aforementioned. I left puzzled.

It was the next day I realized — while watching him look at the newspaper — that it was not what I observed but rather what I felt. I felt a suspension of time around him. A loyalty to something that had — in time — long passed but was ever so present in his mind.

Quite unlike me, I went over to his table. I introduced myself, but there was no response. He looked at that paper, eyes not moving. After a period of time, he touched his watch with his fingers and nodded his head. He turned the paper, his mouth moved, and his face lit up with a smile.

The waitress came over. She smiled at me. She pointed to the Seeing Eye dog — curled near his feet underneath the table — and to his ears. He was deaf.

According to the waitress, the owner of the establishment permitted him to come to the café on a daily basis. Part of his ten percent tithe, she told me. Without fee, he can — she reported — have coffees, croissants (up to five a day) and one meal a day. She told me that he lived in a room above the café and was clothed by the local tailor. Curiously, I comment on the generosity of the community and coming very close to me she informed me that they take care of their own and then walked away.

I returned to the café for the third time, fourth time, and then a fifth time. Day after day he repeated the same actions.

On the sixth day, the owner approached me. He informed me that his guest was really his brother-in-law. His sister had passed away after a long and painful ordeal with cancer.

He informed me that his brother-in-law never left her side and that while they were lowering her casket into the ground, his brother-in-law became deaf and blind. I asked when all of this had occurred and he told me twenty years ago.

Commenting on the touching of the watch with his fingers and the newspaper, the owner smiled. He said that his brother-in-law and his sister would come to the café and read the newspaper to each other. They both enjoyed the Lifestyle section of the paper. The watch, he told me, is for the blind.

When the conversation with the owner stopped, the waitress came to me.

"All he wants is the Lifestyle section of the paper. Kind of strange don't you think. He can't read. He is blind and deaf. Blind and deaf. What does he want with a watch. Everything is given to him."

It was then I connected the feeling I had of him being suspended in time. It now made perfect sense to me. What I was observing was the acts he committed to feel her presence.

There, in the café, he had constructed a space for an activity — which happened a very long time ago — to remain in the present. How could I overlook something so obvious?

For some it is the touch of a gold wedding band, for others a photo, and still for others a wedding song but for the Watch Observer it was a precise moment in time. A moment in time of turning the paper and communication. Without sight and without hearing she — within those activities — was felt totally and absolutely. His deafness and his sightlessness allowed him to only hear and only see her in his mind's eye. All he had to do, at the appropriate time, was turn the paper and give to or receive the reading. I sensed that he communicated the same things he communicated to her when she was alive. He was permitting no earthy distractions.

I left on the eighth day but I — with a surety I have about only a few things — believed that if I returned to that small village and sat in that same café he would be there; the Watch Observer and — unseen by me — his beloved.

My belief did not take into account the new condo development that was erected on that site. I did not even recognize the place when I returned twenty years later.

Left inside me was an uneasy restlessness. I went to the local church, lit candles, and gave a donation. The priest came to me. I inquired about what had happened to the café and the blind, deaf man who looked at the Lifestyle section of the newspaper. The priest was new to the parish and could not answer my questions.

Some stories remain suspended in time, dated in past realities yet oddly present. They will have no conclusion. I leave this story — like the Watch Observer — suspended in time, uncomplete.

Selection

The long black limo drove up to the door
The predator seeking, seeks no more
The door opens, and the children do cry
If there is a God then let us die
The long black limo pulls away,
Back to the house where the pink children play
Black, yellow, brown children, what a delight
Pink children, for now, remain safe at night

The Distraction

"Okay. Okay. I do understand."

"Is there someone with you?"

"Did you just ask me if I have a problem with accepting responsibility?"

"Really! We arranged a certain time."

"Why all of this waiting until the last minute. Surely there is someone who can replace you."

"What?"

"No, I do not think I am too bossy."

"No, I do not think I need to learn assertive skills."

"Really? Really? I hired you! Did you forget that I hired you?"

"Why am I having this conversation with you?"

"You know what, you stay there. I am getting someone else."

"What?"

"Oh, so now you can come. So now you are able to make it!"

"No, I am not paying an additional surcharge. Why should I pay an additional surcharge when this is the time that you were supposed to come."

"You know what?"

"Well, I am going to tell you. This conversation has ended; this is what I am telling you."

"No! No! Now you listen. I am now going to tell you what I am going to do."

"I said, you listen to me! This is what I am going to do. I am going to give all the guests I have waiting to be served the name of your company and email everyone the address of your company. I am then going to use the assertiveness skills I have and while I am serving the food that the catering company has provided I will inform them that you were unable to make it and unable to provide an alternative."

"Yes, that is what I am going to do. And do you know what you can do?"

"Then I will tell you. You can tell that boyfriend of yours to stop making sexual suggestions while we are speaking on the phone. Such conversations are a distraction. I will no longer be requiring your services."

A New Place

He looked around the house. At age sixty-four, how he ached for the life he had when his mother and he lived in the house. Contained within that house was a history of the laughter, tears, and agony of all those years.

He sighed. Granted, if he could, he would turn back the clocks of time and would have encouraged his mother not to take out a loan on the house.

Still, at the time it seemed to be the most sensible thing to do. He certainly was not able to contribute toward the finances. Those doctors, those terrible doctors were the cause of her having to take out a loan on the house. They just kept refusing to put him on a pension. His mother — God bless her soul — understood that he could not work.

Tomorrow the bank was taking over the house. He shuddered to think what his mother would think. All those overtime shifts she worked. All the sacrifices she made. All those holidays she talked about but did not take. He was certain that if she was alive she would have figured out how to save the house.

The lawyer took care of all the funeral arrangements. He was quite sure he could have — if she had just given him the money — done it cheaper. Now here he was saying goodbye to the house.

Suddenly he felt the need to sing one of her favorite hymns, Amazing Grace.

Amazing grace! How sweet the sound
That saved a wretch like me!
I once was lost, but now am found;
Was blind, but now I see

Trying to remember the rest of the hymn he repeated the first part of the hymn again.

Amazing Grace! How sweet the sound
That saved a wretch like me!
I once was lost, but now I am found;
Was blind, but now I see.

It had been a few years since he had gone to church. No other part of the Amazing Grace hymn came to him, so he looked around at the house one more time. Then locking the door behind him, he walked straight across the street and started to live with his Auntie Mable.

The Witness Giver

The first roll of fat — now the largest — was the one that rested on the knees. The texture was soft and mushy. When pressed, it moved in the opposite direction. If you used two hands to try to contain it, well it simply seeped between the fingers or between the hands and hung in suspension. The host called this layer of fat Zuege.

One of the things I want to make clear is that Zuege did not exist before the triangle; nor did Zuege exist before the act of imposition. There was never a hint of Zuege's existence.

Without being too graphic, I will just state that it was the triangle that enacted the imposition. After it had occurred, no matter how invisible the host tried to become, the host felt tasered by the remarks and laughter directed at it.

To ensure — in this story — that there is an accurate account of what occurred, I will inform you that it was during the triangle's imposition that the host first felt tasered. The remarks, the justification, the sworn secrecy, and those various acts inflicted — during that painful electric-like suspension in the air — left the body limp, the mind numb. Zuege was conceived during the imposition by the triangle; it was after the imposition, after the triangle had dispersed, that Zuege was born. The conception happened in the imposition.

Like all that hid, Zuege did not become visible at once. Truth be known, so much went down the toilet bowl that it was a wonder Zuege ever became visible, but what is known for sure is that when Zuege became apparent, Zuege took on a form which refused, absolutely refused, to remain invisible. Zuege, the Witness Giver, became visible. The in-your-face-I-exist Witness Giver. Had this Witness Giver a voice, it would have roared; it would have shrieked.

First, very passively, Zuege obtained new clothing. Satisfied for several years with new sets of clothing there came the day when there was a need for a walker. You would think Zuege would be happy with the walker — the newest model I would add — but no, Zuege was not satisfied with the walker. The walker became useless as Zuege consumed more space. Attached safely to the stomach, resting on the host's knees, Zuege looked at the floor and continued to expand until Zuege dropped over both sides of the host's knees and inched in a forward downward motion to the floor.

Schuld was to say that it was in the lifting of Zuege's host that he first experienced his backache. It would have been better to wait until the lift came but the church was extremely busy, and the casket had to be there at that set time on that day.

People in the church spoke all about Zuege, but no one talked about the triangle. The one they witnessed. It remained a secret in that community.

You think they would have given space for the host of Zuege to speak, but they never did. Their disgust focused on Zuege's visibility and what they — in their silence — had permitted was never the focus of their conversations.

Though Schuld was the first part of the triangle, no one thought that maybe his injury was connected to a little bit of justice. Just like no one thought that justice was done when the other person in the triangle died of alcohol poisoning.

Somewhere — it is unknown exactly why the third part of the triangle confessed — Schuld was arrested. An investigation occurred. It appeared that the triangle during that year had targeted more than just the host of Zuege. Interestingly, fat hung from the stomachs of several of the bodies the triangle had targeted. The various textures of fat (those Witness Givers) were not as aggressive as Zuege but they were there.

Maybe, in time, investigators will have the means to translate what the visibility of the Witness Giver is communicating.

Still, I wonder, is it possible in such a community?

I Ain't Goin' Down No Rabbit Hole

"Damn fool," she thought to herself as he strutted across the road. The red light was blaring at him.

"Damn fool," she muttered to herself as her man lifted his white hat to a motorist who was honking the horn at him.

On the other side of the road, he motioned her to come over. She just kept looking at the light. He turned his back to her and continued walking on the sidewalk, adjusting his white coat and the white belt holding up his white pants.

"Damn fool," she said.

"Lord, you gave me this man," she kept muttering to herself. When the lights turned green, she crossed the road.

Since she was five her Grandmother kept saying, "Watch out for them mens." Every time her Grandmother would warn her, she took the Good Book down from the shelf and read the story of Ananias and Sapphira. "Acts, Chapter 5, verses 1 to 11," her Grandmother would begin and she would have her repeat "I ain't any Sapphria. I ain't goin' to follow no Ananias down no rabbit hole. No sir. I ain't doing that."

Thirty-three years later she recalled what her Grandmother said to her. "I ain't any Sapphria. I ain't going to follow no Ananias down no rabbit hole. No sir. I ain't doing that."

Often, she waited outside the all night poker games in a coffee shop close by or, like today, she followed him around the street waiting for the red lights he crossed to turn green. One thing for sure she knew about this one, he took up a lot of her time. The only thing she never let him interfere with was church time. Her Grandmother taught her that there was no excuse acceptable for messing around with God's time. When her Grandmother was alive they went to church every Sunday.

She heard about but never met her grandmother's daughter (her Mama). Her father, according to her Grandmother, was taken care of by the government.

"His head got busted up," explained her grandmother. "It's not like he doesn't want to be with you," she said to her. "It's just that his head got busted up and theys got to keep him locked up in the loony bin."

She saw him once. Upon seeing him, she called out to him the name Papa and he came right up to her.

"Gotta smoke?" he said looking at her.

"Papa," she said again.

"Yah, ok kid, as long as you got a smoke, I'll be your Papa."

She gave him the cigarette and he reached over and took the pack. Walking down the corridor he yelled out "Let that be a lesson to you kid," and then he laughed.

Grandmother kept insisting that underneath all of that meanness he loved her. "Just can't follow him down the rabbit hole," she said. "Can't follow him down the rabbit hole."

The preacher was kind to her when her Grandmother died. He got her a room in a rooming house and that is where she met Ned. He and his white suits and white top hats. He looked grand.

Within a week they were married.

In the beginning Ned went to church with her but after they moved out of the rooming house into their own subsidized apartment he stopped going to church with her. It made no sense to her that he would stop going to church. The words of her Grandmother come back to her. "Don't be no Sapphira. Don't you be no Sapphira. Don't follow him down the rabbit hole," so she continued — without him — going to church.

Buddy was big. He was so big that sometimes, not too many times, he got stuck in the door. It was a Monday when Buddy came to the door.

"Where's Ned?"

"Sleeping."

"Where?"

"Will bring you to him."

Muttering to herself she repeated, "Don't be no

Sapphira. Don't you be no Sapphira. Don't follow him down the rabbit hole."

"Ned," says Buddy, "yous too late now." He then took out a club and started smashing up Ned's face.

"Ain't no Sapphira," she said and finding the pan underneath the kitchen sink she filled it up with hot water.

"I'm finished here now," said Buddy.

"OK," she said.

"Lord you gave me this man," she muttered as she washed the dishes. A groan came from Ned and nothing more.

She heard a siren. Someone must have called the police. Maybe it was a neighbour, maybe it was Buddy using the scene to send a message to others who were behind on their dues. You never knew. You just never knew what was real.

"Ain't no Sapphira," she told the police officer as she was drying off the dishes. "I ain't following him down the rabbit hole."

She looked at the police officer and she knew what was going to happen. Same thing that happened to her Papa was the same thing happening to her man now. She happened to glance at herself in the mirror and turned to look at herself directly.

"This time," she said to herself, "I'm not giving him my smokes." Then she gave herself a big smile and an authority came into her voice, "No sir, not me. I ain't goin' down no rabbit hole."

The Journey of Deleted Pathways

She looked at me wondering if I knew. At this time in my life, I did know. I spent a lot of time carefully organizing the words so she would not know I knew.

Somehow, I had the wisdom to not give her my story. I did not give her the text nor allow her to rearrange the words for her monetary gain.

All my writing life, I had viewed her as someone who had guarded the process of how the words travelled into text and from the text into the various stories. It never occurred to me to question or secure the ownership of the words, or the text, or the various stories. Where did I learn to betray myself and my stories in such a manner?

Somewhere, I am not too sure when, a doubt occurred. I do not know where it came from. Maybe it was a smirk I saw on her face that triggered the doubt or maybe it was something that gleamed out of her eye just before she winked it. I don't know and truth be known I really do not want to know.

What I know is that my words had to be protected. I did not confront her but I did provide her with dry, arid words, which she took for moisture and substance. Any word she placed in her story was at risk of being misrepresented. My words had to be protected. I knew when I replaced them with dry, arid words that those same words upon investigation or inquiry would be so brittle that when they were reviewed they would collapse into ashes. Only soot would be left. I knew she would be left with nothing to build upon or sustain.

I decided to put my words into a yarn of texts that knitted themselves into a coded story. I thought to myself that I should have done this decades ago. Some things just take time.

It took time to unravel the self-betrayal. In a safe place I decoded the story, taking the time I needed to rewind the yarn and knit the words together in some type of authenticity from which the story could evolve. It did so cautiously.

I saw her — after the decoding — off and on. She had someone else lined up. I felt hurt that I was so easily replaced. When washed with this type of self-pity, I knew I was longing for the days of my former innocence. I looked at her stunning beauty and I wanted so desperately to believe that her smile and welcome had to do with missing me and not the incredible monetary value my words had brought into my life, but I had learned differently. The innocence was gone.

So I smiled and provided even drier arid words and she smiled very hopefully. The difference being I knew and she did not know I knew.

This time when we parted I felt the freshness of the air. My lungs inhaled deeply. Truly — with earnestness — I have to tell you that until that moment I was not aware that she consumed the oxygen around me. I did not know that I was in a painful existence, gasping for air.

My life — I became aware — was not intended to be a gasping painful existence. This oxygen extinguisher had to go. Having her around — even in small dosages — was just too painful, just too painful; so I said goodbye and deleted — mid sentence — all journeyed pathways.

The White Brown Girl

Mama

Mama had two daughters. One of the daughters had thin, "white," English lips and straight, fine, comb-through hair. Her pencil skirt fit without any protrusions. The other daughter had thick lips and frizzy, coarse hair but she passed. Thunder Bay had lots of people like that.

Still, Mama always had the fear. Her Mama done had the fear. Her Mama's Mama done had the fear. That's why the women (where she came from) were always prepared. Hangings do that to you.

At a very early age Mama saw her cousin (on her Granddaddy's side) hung. The cousin had the thick lips, the frizzy hair ("the fool didn't know enough to braid it," thought Mama as she watched her cousin swing from the rope), and the protruding backside. It was then that Mama (in her mind) connected no traits to no hangings.

So you can imagine what Mama felt when she saw the protrusion of her daughter's backside. The protrusion, for Mama, was like a lightning rod. In a flash, the protrusion aligned those thick lips and coarse hair to her Granddaddy's people. "No daughter of mine," thought Mama, "is going to be hung."

Immediately, Mama set out to do the preparations of the plan. The preparations had been, up until that time, what Mama called "just-in-case preparations." (All her Mama's people had the preparations done to them; that's how Mama ended up in Thunder Bay.) Anyone can have a plan not to be hung, but all those little preparations made sure you weren't hung. One of the preparations her cousin forgot was to have the hair braided. "Everyone knew you had to have the hair braided," grumbled Mama.

Mama, until her last breath, kept repeating the preparations. They were simple. Most of the preparations of the plan had to do with praises. Every time her daughter with the traits did something for the daughter without the traits, Mama praised her. Mama would tell her how strong she was, what a good girl she was, and how proud she was of her. Mama praised her so much that it got to the point where her daughter with the traits figured that it was just natural to help her sister. After a while, the sister without the traits got this feeling of entitlement.

After Mama Died

After Mama died the two sisters remained in the house that Mama had bought from the settlement. Their Daddy had a terrible accident. The accident killed him right away. Mama said it was a blessing he died quickly. "Never had no trouble with the Company," Mama had told them.

The sister without the traits got married. It was decided by the sisters that he would move in with them. This way, the sisters did not have to live apart in different places.

The sister with the traits kept on helping the sister without the traits. In the beginning he asked the sister with the traits if she would mind making his lunch and washing the odd shirt or boxer shorts. Very soon he was no longer asking. There seemed to be an unsaid agreement that whatever was done for his wife would also be done for him.

The girl with the traits never thought anything of it. It was taught in church that the two shall become one so ... what was some extra laundry and plates of food.

When the children were born, her sister told her of the nasty germs in the daycare. How relieved the sister without the traits and her husband were to know that the girl with the traits would be taking care of the children. The children adored their Auntie and she loved them as her own.

The Shifting

One day while ironing and watching TV, the girl with the traits saw (on TV) a dog biting someone, water being sprayed on a group of people, crosses being burned in front of churches, people hanging from branches, and massive groups of people marching.

"What's that about?" asked the girl with the traits.

"Oh, that's nothing," said the girl without the traits. "It's all got to do with where Mama's people come from. Got nothing to do with us up here."

The girl without the traits turned off the TV. Immediately, the girl with the traits turned the TV back on. As she looked at the images on the TV, a deep shifting occurred within the very bottom of her belly. When she returned to the ironing board, the shifting feeling (way deep in the bottom of her belly) vanished.

The next day she was shopping at the grocery store. The clerk asked her if she would like to enter a contest. "You could win a two-week all-inclusive vacation," said the clerk. While telling the clerk that she never won anything, the girl with the traits quickly answered the skill-testing questions, folded the paper, and put it into the contest box.

By the time she had driven the car — with the back seat full of groceries — home, she had forgotten all about the contest.

About two or three weeks later the phone rang. "Hey, you got a phone call," said the sister without the traits.

"Oh?" asked the girl with the traits.

"We," said the voice, "would like to inform you that you have won a contest."

"What? What contest?" asked the girl with the traits.

"The one you entered a few weeks back," said the voice. "You have won a two-week all-inclusive Caribbean vacation."

"Really? When is it?" asked the girl with the traits.

Her question, unknown to the voice, was a very important one. For you see, the only time she could leave her sister was when her sister and her sister's husband rented a cottage for two weeks. (The kids loved the cottage, and upon returning to their home would run into the house to tell their Auntie all about their "adventures.") As luck would have it, the vacation she had won was during that time.

The Reconciling

About four days into the vacation, she happened to get a glimpse of herself in the bevelled lounge mirror. "How did I get so brown?" she asked herself.

She was surprised at how much her body liked the heat; by the seventh day the hue of her skin was a dark chocolate brown.

One day, coming out of the pool, she unbraided her hair to dry it. Her hair sprung out all over her head. Late for dinner, she had no time to braid it back and went to the dining room with her hair unbraided. She got so many compliments about her hair and her head felt so comfortable that she left her hair unbraided for the whole vacation.

Magazines, which you did not have to pay for, were in the lounge. While waiting for the entertainment to start she picked up one of the free magazines. There, on the front cover of the magazine, were the pictures she had seen on TV.

While looking at the pictures, she heard a voice. "Shameful that, what they are doing!" said a voice. "Shameful thing!" She looked up to see who was speaking to her. There, in front of her, stood a man with globs of cream on his bright pink burnt face. She looked into his eyes and all that was present, in those eyes, was an embarrassed compassion. "Think you will be okay here. Am quite sure you are safe here," he said, patting her shoulder as he walked by. The pat on the shoulder felt warm.

"Okay? Safe? What on earth is he talking about?" she asked herself.

He disappeared around the corner before she could ask him anything.

The bevelled mirror just happened to be beside where he exited. She caught her reflection in it at the same time the magazine fell off her lap onto the floor. Reaching to pick up the magazine (the image of herself still in her mind), her eyes looked at the pictures. Suddenly there was recognition.

The images of the pictures and the image of herself melded. The shifting — that she had first felt after she had had the conversation with her sister and turned the TV back on — shot up from the pit of her stomach, sending shock waves up and down her body. It slammed into every cell of her body with such force that she hit the back of the chair with a thud and slumped down into the chair.

The entertainment was playing when she gained awareness. She sat there, unable to move. Her mind now understood the embarrassed, compassionate eyes, the stranger's words, her sister's voice identifying Mama's people. She understood how it was all linked to her. She thought up her preparations during the flight back home. She tightly, very tightly, braided her hair before entering the house. The plan had to do with restitution.

The Restitution

While giving her sister with the traits a load of laundry to do, the sister without the traits asked about her all-inclusive vacation. "Get me a beer, will ya!" hollered a voice down the stairs. Without waiting for the girl with the traits to reply, her sister rushed to the fridge, grabbed one of the beers, and rushed upstairs.

The girl with the traits took the load of laundry and then dropped the basket by the washing machine. As the laundry piled up, it became noticeable that there was some type of outer shifting going on.

Nothing was said about things not being done. There were lot of looks and glares, but nothing was said. It was not until after one of the children ran out into the street that words were spoken.

Servants were hired and servants were fired. The sister without the traits always found something wrong with the people hired to do the various jobs the girl with the traits had done all of those years. Finally there was an agreement. The agreement was as follows:

1. All the laws in place for domestic help in Canada would be adhered to.
2. The basement would be renovated and would meet all the requirements of a legal daycare.
3. All the cost of the renovations would be absorbed by the family of the sister without the traits.
4. No rent would be charged for the space.
5. All income from the daycare would belong to the sister with the traits: her sister without the traits and the sister's husband could have none of the income.

The girl with the traits let it be known that all this was restitution for all the years of unpaid labour. The sister with the traits was pleased. Her sister, the one without the traits, felt abandoned.

Initially, the husband of the sister without the traits felt a mixture of anger and puzzlement. He was later heard telling a friend of his that his sister-in-law had had some type of hormonal problem, but that it had all got worked out.

Years stretched into decades. After the last child had left home, both sisters agreed that it was time to separate and sell the house. Each received half of the profits.

The sister with the traits settled in Winnipeg. She bought a three-storey house near a park and church. The children in the area liked going to her daycare.

Upon reaching seventy-five years of age, she decided to travel. She had a wonderful time. Her unbraided hair developed speckles of grey. On her eightieth birthday, she packed her bags and flew to Thunder Bay.

Forgiveness

She was pleased to see that the graveyard was in such good condition. Mama, she knew, would be pleased.

Slowly she knelt in front of the grave, and patting it ever so lightly, she said, "Mama, you don't got to worry no more. No dogs, Mama, bit me. No rope hung around this white brown girl's neck, Mama. My home never got burned, Mama. My church, Mama, never got burned. No burning crosses, Mama, in my front yard. No burning crosses in my church front yard, Mama. You rest now, Mama. I am eighty years old; you can rest now, Mama. You don't got to worry no more, Mama! You don't got to worry no more!"

Then, placing her cheek to the grave, she whispered, "I knows what you did, Mama! I knows what you did, Mama! I loves you, Mama. Loves … you … Mama."

Then she slowly got up, adjusted her coat, and walked away.

Whisper Spirits

They turn to the window
Whisper spirits

Gliding in and out
Whisper spirits

They sit so upright
Whisper spirits

Never leaving their seat
Whisper spirits

Never leaving their seat
They sit so upright
Gliding in and out
They turn to the window
Whisper spirits

Is that what the memories are
Whisper spirits

Is that where they are lodged
Whisper spirits

Is that where they eat and play and love
Whisper spirits

Is that where you are
Whisper spirits

Is this where you are
Eating and playing and loving
Lodged
In the memories
Whisper spirits

For God is loving
Whisper spirits

At 3am in the morning
Whisper spirits

I welcome you
Whisper spirits

It is so nice to form this reunion
Whisper spirits

It is so nice
To form this reunion
I welcome you
At 3am in the morning
For God is loving
Whisper spirits

It is time to sleep
Whisper spirits

You keep looking through the window
Whisper spirits

Seated so upright
Whisper spirits

Celebrating this reunion
Whisper spirits

Celebrating this reunion
Seated so upright
You keep looking through the window
It is time to sleep
Whisper spirits

Good night whisper spirits
Good night.

Unknown to Known

Pat did not like the uniqueness of being an alcoholic. The gifts that emerged were welcomed but to be powerless over a liquid substance was embarrassing. "I have an allergy," stated Pat. Another bottle of gold liquid descended down his throat.

Now that the ink in the pen was frozen, he was no longer able to draw. Moving his body deeper into the sleeping bag he placed the pen and paper at the bottom of the sleeping bag. The winds blew fearlessly around the bus stop shelter. "People should give long johns," thought Pat. Quickly he zipped up the sleeping bag, leaving a small part around his face unzipped.

When he awoke, he felt a warmth surround him. "God, this is nice," he thought. Very soon the warmth turned into a prickly feeling and then the prickly feeling started to hurt him. He felt as if something was burning him and yelled for help. No one heard him. If they did, they did not come over and help him unzip the stuck zipper.

It was several years later that the arsonist was charged with Pat's murder. The newspaper printed a picture of Pat's face and an article — which referred to him as a "street artist" — about him was written. People started to buy his art.

It is amazing how, sometimes, the unknown becomes the known.

The Firing

Did I just see a distance in your eye? The one you use to dismiss the servants from the room.

Surely you understood that I had to clean the spot on the carpet. You know that! Yes, I am sure you know that. The shirt — the one I ironed — had to be done by myself. I mean it was obvious! The wrinkles were unacceptable. Imagine a person of your status wearing a wrinkled shirt. The dishes, of course, were caked. I agreed with you there. I did not think you realized that they had to be rewashed.

Yes, that is exactly what I am telling you! They had to be rewashed. All of those stuck particles on newly washed plates. You saw the particles on the rims. Parts of the rims could no longer be defined. Not knowing where the rims of the plates start or end, it is ridiculous!

You say we can afford to hire people to clean up. You say it is not becoming that I — your partner — should be cleaning up after people. At the same time you say this: you tell me all the firings of the servants are not necessary.

Don't you get it? The firing is my frustration. You keep hiring and leave me to fire. I am always having to fire those you hire. I am always the one to wipe their tears. I hate this. No more. I am stopping.

What do I mean stopping? I mean that from now I will not fire anyone. No one.

You know me when I get this way.

Excuse me? What do you mean, what will you do when you use them up?

Suspenders and a Belt

Talking to his companion, who was eating the bread crumbs off his plate, he wondered about his mother. The chemotherapy had not helped her.

When his father died, he took the belt his father gave him and put it around his waist. The fact that his suspenders held up his pants perfectly fine was irrelevant. His father gave him the belt as a present, before he died, and that was all that mattered.

He told his companion this. The companion appeared uninterested and kept eating. When he left the kitchen, his companion walked down the leg of the table. He wondered where his companion was rushing to in such a hurry. Looking at his watch, he rushed towards the hospital.

Entering his mother's hospital room, he saw a smile on her lips. She expressed, between breathes, her joy that she would soon be seeing his father. Jealousy consumed him.

There had always been places, with his parents, he was never invited. Places full of happiness. During those times he was not invited into their space, a sense of aloneness tiptoed him into isolation.

The servants, when he was a child, were kind but they too had their places full of happiness that he was not invited into.

As a child and teenager, he told himself that his feelings of isolation and aloneness made sense. He told himself that all children without siblings experienced what he experienced. As an adult, he noticed that those thoughts were no longer a source of comfort for him.

The weight of depression surrounded his body like a coat. The weight of the coat varied but no matter what he did, it refused to leave his body. In the presence of his companion the depression surrounded him like a very light spring jacket. Somehow, it did not bother him that his companion never talked back to him or initiated a conversation. It simply did not matter.

Now in the hospital room, the weight of the depression felt like a very, very heavy layered winter coat. His feet — a recent new sensation that had entered his body — felt as if they were nailed to the floor. He simply could not move toward her.

She died smiling at him.

Several hours later, he was in the parking space. A gentle thought came to him that it was time to remove his father's belt. He did not question it. As the belt descended into the garbage can, air exited his body with such a force it roared and was immediately replaced by a wounded howl. People around him ran towards their cars. By the time he got home his body felt so light that he actually questioned whether or not he was floating. Though the sensation was very welcome, he — given her recent death — thought it to be strange.

When he got home, his companion had invited others to eat the food on the plates. This time, their lack of attentiveness bothered him. The bothersome feeling lodged itself in the back of his throat. A growl sound escaped through his teeth. A few companions stopped eating.

The events of the day had tired him and he decided that a good nap would remove the feeling. It did not. As a matter of fact the feeling magnified itself. He thought it to be strange.

Finding himself at the hardware store, he asked for a can of roach spray and was given two cans. He bought both of them. For the next two days, neighbours in his apartment building complained about all the roaches that entered their apartment. They demanded, from the landlord, to know where the infestation came from. The landlord told them that he had no idea. The exterminators were brought in. By the end of the second week, the whole building was sprayed. One resident, in disgust, left.

With the roaches gone he became aware of all the dirty dishes, the sticky floor, and the grime coating the walls and windows. By the time he was finished cleaning and renovating, the hardware store manager and himself were on a first-name basis. He soon got to know the names of the storekeepers. Contentment was a word he started using to describe his existence.

The following year he got rid of his suspenders.

An Agreed Upon Time

You know, my beloved, I don't mind that your grey hair is falling over your shoulder. I don't even mind the jaggedness of your nails. I do mind, my beloved, the slurring of your words.

Seriously, how am I to know? How am I to know? The agreed upon time is approaching and I want to make sure.

The other day, as I was watching you sleep, you looked so peaceful and rested. I thought it was the perfect time. I thought it was the perfect time to take the pillow we have chosen and gently place it over your mouth and nose. A tension inside of me poked its way into existence. "It is time, lift the pillow," it whispered to me. Even now, I think it a bit strange that such thoughts and feelings were present.

One month, three days, and twenty-two hours; that is the agreed upon time. After sixty years of being together what is another month, three days, and twenty-two hours?

I think I will go to the corner store and buy some milk for us.

Done with You

Here I am at the kitchen table writing a letter to you, while you are sleeping in that bed you insisted that we purchase forty-three years ago.

Four months ago, you came into our home with Chris. After I had poured the tea into all three teacups, you took the teapot and quietly said (looking directly into my eyes), "Done. I'm done."

Then (taking Chris's hand in yours), you walked to the door and you turned around, walked towards me and took my hand. Placing your wedding band in the palm of my hand, you said, "I'm going to live with Chris now. I'll get all my stuff tomorrow." Then, you folded the fingers of my hand around the ring.

But you know all of that!

What you may not know is how I reacted. So, I will tell you. I picked up the teacups and saucers (one at a time), and I brought them to the kitchen, starting with Chris's teacup. I then washed each cup and plate slowly and patted the cups and saucers (starting with the ones that were for me) dry. Then I went to sleep.

And when I woke up, I went for a walk. I kept thinking that I should be reacting, but nothing was happening. Well (no, that's not completely true), something did happen once. It happened when a thought came to me that I must tell the children (you remember our children) — all four of them — what had occurred. Yup, it did come to me that I should tell the children what had occurred. But then, another thought came to me, "Why the hell should I tell the children! I didn't leave! He did!" So, I never did tell the children. Each time they called, I simply told them that you were not there and to contact you by your cellphone. They never heard from me what happened, and I know they did not hear from you because they would have told me. They never did tell me, and they always tell me things. Always!

Oh, I hear you stirring. Yup, there you are stirring in the bed. Mmmm, there you go gritting your teeth. You'll be up soon. What to do? What to do?

Last night, I heard a knocking at the door. I went to the door and opened it and there you were. After four months, there you were at the door. You told me that you were "done with Chris," that it was "something that happened. Probably a mid-life crisis," you said.

What you did not know is that my mind was empty of you, my emotions empty of you, my spirit empty of you, but my body betrayed me. You gave me that look — that look that only you can — and my body reached to your arms.

This morning I lay in your arms waiting for the satisfaction, the comfort, the completeness my body has had from you for forty-three years minus four months. There was nothing. Nothing.

I lay in your arms, empty. Slowly, I removed your arms wrapped around me and quietly left the bed. My body liked the distance. I checked everywhere (everywhere inside of me), and I now know that I am empty of you.

So, this is what I'm going to do.

In a few minutes, I will put this letter in an envelope and I will put the envelope on top of the fridge. And when you awake, I will make tea for two, and we will read the *New York Times* — share and laugh — as we have done for forty-three years minus four months. Then, when you have left, I will take the envelope off the fridge — change all the locks on all the doors — and nail this envelope (with this letter inside) to the front door.

When that is done, I will slip my wedding band of forty-three years off my finger, place it on the nail that is securing the envelope to the door, and write on the envelope in bright red ink for all to see these words: DONE WITH YOU.

Then I will close the door, walk to the kitchen, and make a cup of tea for one.

In the Passing

Where did you go?
In the passing…

I want to know!
In the passing…

How selfish can you be?
In the passing…

Leaving your life and me.
In the passing...

I long to lie by your side,
in the passing.

To retreat to your arms and confide,
in the passing.

I long to smell your sweet sweat,
in the passing.

I long to inhale your sweet breath,
in the passing.

But since I have decided not to die,
in the passing…

I have decided to say goodbye.
in the passing…

I will not miss,
in the passing…

the price of a kiss.
in the passing…

I will not miss,
in the passing…

the cocaine on my lips,
in the passing…

I will continue to receive the grace,
in the passing…

to stay and walk in this place.

The Man with the Hound Dog Face

"Chickecaw, chickecaw, chick, chick! Chickecaw, chickecaw, chick, chick!" The man with the hound dog face, the man with the hound dog face, he hollered at the moon, and he cursed at the moon, and he screeched at the moon. He hollered, and he hollered, and he hollered! He cursed! He cursed! He cursed! He screeched! He screeched! He screeched, and then he howled! He howled!

Silence. Silence. Silence … silence.

I climbed up the hill. I climbed, climbed, climbed, climbed up the hill and I saw him — bathed in moonbeams, bathed in moonbeams — not moving, not moving.

I ran down the hill, ran, ran, ran and I came to the door, door, door and I knocked at the door and it opened.

And I said, "He's not moving! He's not moving!"

And the voice said, "I don't care!" And the door slammed shut.

I ran, ran, ran to the police station, and I said to the police person, I said, "He's not moving! He's not moving!"

The police person and I ran past the door, up the hill and there he was. The moonbeams lined in a row, sitting beside him. Those cursed moonbeams lined in a row, sitting beside him!

Three days later, I read in the newspaper,

"Renowned physicist found dead in the bush — died of alcohol poisoning. Daughter only person who attended the funeral."

And when I read that, I ran. I ran past the door, climbed up the hill, and I cursed at the moon! I screeched at the moon! I hollered at the moon! I cursed, cursed, cursed! I screeched, screeched, screeched! I hollered, hollered, hollered!

And the moon said, "I don't want you! I do *not* want *you*! I don't want you!"

And I asked, "You don't want me? *You*, you don't want me? You don't want me?"

And I ran, ran, ran down the hill and I knocked, knocked, knocked on the door and the door opened and crying, I said, "The moon doesn't want me! The moon doesn't want me!"

And the voice said, "If you return here you must keep the door shut, shut, shut, shut." So, I went in and I shut the door, and I cried to that place of silence.

And then in the silence I heard It on the other side of the door: "Chickecaw, chickecaw, chick, chick! Chickecaw, chickecaw, chick, chick! Chickecaw, chickecaw, chick, chick!"

And the voice said, "If you open the door you will leave this lifestyle."

So ... I didn't open the door. The door was never opened by me again. And I have kept it shut ever since.

And sometimes It visits the door and leaves again and that makes sense to me. It makes perfect sense to me. For I am, you see, the daughter of the man with the hound dog face. I am she, and It knows that.

Once Again, Sound Rescues Truth

Sound had the ability to travel past, future, or stay in the present. Part (well really quite a large part) of Sound's responsibilities was to defend, protect, and sustain Truth.

One day, Sound was travelling on the vibration waves and heard a faint whisper. Unable to make out all the words, Sound sought clarification from Vastness, and then waited. When Vastness responded, Sound fully understood the words. They caused Sound a great deal of anxiety! Usually Sound was not very excitable, but these words were different. In its excitement Sound — atypically — demanded from Vastness the location and the source of the words. Vastness refused. Something truly was wrong.

Usually Vastness was not so rude.

The excitement within Sound evolved into a frantic form of panic! Without a doubt, Sound knew that something definitely was wrong. Zigzagging back and forth between past, present, and future, Sound sought the words. It was the third time revisiting the past that Sound finally found Truth. There in the depth of the past — surrounded by Thickness — Sound found Truth.

Truth (usually quite jubilant) appeared exhausted and worn from the struggle to find an exit.

A sense of duty, mixed with compassion, replaced the frantic panic within Sound. Persistently and determinedly, Sound burrowed through Thickness. Each movement towards Truth created a channel, one that Thickness (though Thickness tried) could not collapse.

Eventually Sound connected with Truth, and they moved up through the channel that Sound had created. Up and up they went and finally exited. When they emerged from Thickness, Truth (sustained and protected by Sound) slowly but surely regained strength.

Jeep Drivers

Faces, encased in lines, move beside the jeep. Dust blows, zigzagging through the rocks. Streams have dried up. Screams are heard from the bodies littered around. Here food develops hands and chokes the inner lining of the throat. Maggots are sucked for the fluid of their bodies. In this place, blood is relished for its nutrients and the way it pulsates down the throat.

The ancient ones warned us, but no one listened. Now that the prediction has come to pass, those with faces encased with lines walk beside the jeep searching for shade. The others focus on survival. Very few drive the jeep.

Behind the Soft Black Eyes

Often she wondered if Nela knew. Nela who washed her feet. Nela who washed her hands. Nela whose beautiful skin was replaced by thin lines that etched themselves along the outside of Nela's body. How she adored the brittle gray hair that eventually replaced Nela's beautiful black hair.

She laughed to herself. Oh, how she wished she would be around to see the look on Nela's face when the will was read. The thought of the pain that would surely pierce Nela's heart brought a warmth to her ninety-year-old body. It also fueled the warm, soft ember glow in her black eyes.

He always sided with Nela. She was left at home while Nela and he went to the opera, to the concerts, to the plays. She was his favorite one. You'd think that Nela was his wife. Disrespectful child.

It was always about Nela. Nela in the psychiatric ward. Nela overdosing with pills. Nela pregnant. Imagine that slut pregnant at the age of fourteen. And he crying the way he did when their daughter miscarried? That damn child was always the centre of his attention.

She needed her pillow fixed and called Nela's name; there was no response. It was the grandchild who found Nela dead in her bed.

When the grandchild and her son told her what happened to Nela something occurred that no one in the family could have foreseen. The warm, soft ember glow in her black eyes turned into glowing coals; the kind you see in the inhabitants of hell pictured in some of the religious books.

Within a matter of a few days, she had to be taken to the hospital and placed in a locked ward. Everyone believed that her ravings about Judgment Day and burning in hell were signs of the depth of her grief for Nela.

One day someone found the following letter tucked under the bottom of Nela's jewelry box. The following was noted:

"Dearest Mother,

I have been told that I will not be able to care for you much longer. The heart disease I have is not curable, and it will eventually kill me. I want you to know that I have always understood that you had no knowledge of what Dad did to me. It took me many years to realize this.

You see Mother, I believed all the stories he told me about you. Even though I believed him at the time, I want you to know that I never stopped loving you.

Now that I am dead I want you to know that his death was not accidental. I did not want another child with him. I was so scared to tell you because he told me how fragile you were and that you would end up like Grandmother.

I put the pills you took for your nerves into the soda he was drinking, and I think that is what caused the car accident. Forgive me.

Your loving daughter,

Nela"

For another ten years, she lived, and no one showed her the letter. They spoke about Nela and how courageous she was. Some compared her to a martyr. The more they told her how much Nela loved her, the more she raged.

After a while the visits stopped. They simply could not endure her hatred for poor, dear Nela.

Along with the residents of the ward, she plotted how she was going to kill Nela in heaven. Everyone in the ward agreed that God would approve.

Before the Shared Path

If you came to me
On the night we planned
I would whisper into the sea shell land
Full of grit and toil
Full of wastage spoil
I would present the pearl
Of the former girl

If you came to me
On the night we planned
I would whisper into the sea shell land
Full of grit and toil
Full of wastage spoil
I would present the girl
Of the pom-pom twirl

But you came to me
During a sunlit day
All visible during this month of May
And I cannot hide behind the midnight sea

Nor stop the sun from shining on me
Fear strikes my heart and when I realize
You are here standing right by my side

Is it the love I love of the old past
Is it the love of memories on the sunlit beach
Is it the love conversations we had without speech
Are you pining for the days of old
Wanting to step out of a life that is so cold
Are you here to say that you are going to stay
Or is it simply a cup of coffee as you go your way

My mind is racing, and you reach for my hand
I feel the excitement of your warm touch
Then I look at your body and see the unfamiliar crouch
Your lines on your face are very visible to me
And I realize now that it's both of us that see
So we talk, and we share of those long ago years
Then we take that first step down the path that we both will share

Daya

He had told her that they could separate and that he would rejoin her at the usual location. He assured her that he understood her need for the separation. The fact that Daya was sick — he acknowledged — was a challenge.

The majority of her emotional support came from Daya. Only a slight amount of the support she needed came from him. Daya was the faithful one. Daya was there through all the breakups. Daya was the trusted one, the one who always waited for her. Daya was the one who took such pity on her and would nuzzle up to her.

Her heart now sunk at the thought of Daya. She cupped Daya's face into her hand. She placed her forehead against Daya's forehead and instructed the veterinarian to proceed with the injection. After Daya had passed, she climbed upon the table and using her whole body — she held Daya for the last time.

The sunlight hit her face when she left the veterinarian's office. Her world felt void. She met him at the usual place. He smiled, ordered for them the espresso he liked and proceeded to take her to a destination that lacked — for her — support and company.

She was now his Daya. He no longer had to share her. It was worth all the money he paid. He texted a reminder to himself to get rid of the evidence.

The Weight Loser

She realized that she had enough — not of the person mind you — but of the raging alcoholic. It was an entity upon itself.

Oh, that self-serving raging alcoholic fed off her anxieties and smiled with glee as the age lines formed on her face. The raging alcoholic, before and after possessing her, presented her with cream-filled donuts and cheesecake. Cream-filled donuts and cheesecake which transported her into a world of a gingerbread house surrounded by an adorable hard white and pink icing fence. In that world she did not know whether it was Monday, Tuesday, or Wednesday; it always felt like a weekend.

Amazed at the scales not budging, she finally heard her body. It told her in no uncertain terms that her life was weighted. She wondered with what.

The self-serving raging alcoholic went away on a business trip. Walking to the bus stop, she saw an enormous person in a jogging outfit. Looking at the faces of the people moving out of the way for the individual, some people had smiles of encouragement on their faces, and others were smirking. The person jogged by them and smiled back to the supportive people and appeared to ignore the ones smirking.

She started jogging the next day. The following day after jogging, she began reading self-help books. She watched YouTube videos on relaxation exercises.

The raging alcoholic returned. She took a bite of the cream-filled donuts and cheesecake but only a bite. She felt a discomfort in her body; the same uneasiness she got when a distressed baby was left unattended.

It was soon after this that she dismantled the gingerbread house and the hard white and pink icing fence. "How?" you may ask. The answer is she poured boiling lemon water on them.

The raging alcoholic at first found the inability to please her with cream-filled donuts and cheesecake a bit unsettling. The more she unloaded the weight of life and placed it firmly on the shoulders of the raging alcoholic the lighter she became.

In desperation to keep the rage going, the raging alcoholic tried to feed others. Some took a bite of the cream-filled donuts and cheesecake, others consumed them, but the majority of people told the raging alcoholic that they were not interested.

Disappointed at no longer being able to feed upon her, the raging alcoholic stayed with her in the hope that one day she would come to her senses. She never did.

Driving on the Rims of God's Eyelashes

I was left driving on the rim of God's eyelashes, supported by darkness.

I was left driving on the rim of God's eyelashes, supported by God's vision.

I was left driving on the rim of God's eyelashes, supported by God's love.

I was left driving on the rim of God's eyelashes, supported by God's grace.

The Young Little Dog

According to the newspaper clipping, a person, in a fit of rage, had taken a large hunting knife and sliced a child in quarters. Still angry, the murderer slid the knife across the table and shouted to a young little dog to get his gizzards. The dog ran towards the flesh scattered on the side of the table. It was then — according to the murderer — that she ran towards the dog. She kicked the dog's stomach with such force, the dog slumped to the floor unable to move. According to the murderer she had no right to kick the dog. It was a good dog, just doing what it was told. The dog was kicked by the wife of the murderer.

The newspaper article reported that after she had kicked the dog, she collected all the body parts of their child and looked in the direction of her husband with such defiance and malice a dark deep fear sprung up in him.

The murderer — the husband — then told the reporter that after she had given him the look he felt pinned to something. Struggle, according to the killer, was useless. He just could not move. According to the husband, for her to do that to him meant she had some magical powers.

It was his opinion that there was no need for that young little dog to die. She could have, he said, saved the dog by using her magical powers and she did not. Shame, according to the husband, was all hers because she did not save the dog. She knew, he said, what he would do. She should have left when his cousin told him what he did to her.

According to the husband, she went right strange. He said that once she had all the baby's parts, she organized them like a jigsaw puzzle. Putting the head of their child on the one hand and cradling the body of their child in her arms, she rested the pieces of the child's body on her body.

While the blood oozed through her fingers and between her arms, she rocked and sang to their child. The sound of her voice got into the ears of a nearby police person. The murderer — her husband — was arrested and jailed. She — after having to forcibly open her hand and arms — ended up being put in an insane asylum where she died by her hand a few months later.

According to the newspaper article, up until this day, the community remains upset about what happened. When her husband goes to the restaurant, they pat him on the back while buying him beers. Yes, they are still talking about that poor little young dog. She had no right, according to them, to kick that dog. You see the dog did no wrong. Such a shame what she did, such a shame.

Maler and the Troll

Once upon a time, a very long time ago there lived a troll. A long-finger-nailed, green skinned, grey-eyed, sharp jagged toothed, big-foot troll. When he sang, he was adorable, absolutely adorable. People loved to hear him sing but when he was not singing, he sat on the sidewalk.

Now Maler — whose family had lived for generations in the village — started to wonder why the troll lived on the sidewalk. He asked the troll. The troll said he did not know. He asked the people who gathered to hear the troll sing. The people who gathered to listen to the troll sing reported that they did not know. He asked the mayor, and the mayor said he did not know. He asked the judge, and the judge said he did not know.

It was a Tuesday, a bitterly cold day. Raindrops the size of the top of your thumb fell from the sky. Yes, that is what I said. The raindrops were as big as the top of your thumb. So forceful were those raindrops that wherever they touched the body, bruises came up.

Everyone ran into their homes; except for the troll. The troll had no home. He was exposed to the rain.

Several bruises appeared on his face, hands and other parts of his body. Poor troll. Poor, poor troll.

Maler's parents had taught him that people make their fate. Maler was not comfortable with this belief. He looked at the troll and aware that the troll had no control over the weather, Maler decided to approach the troll about his living conditions. The troll was very suspicious about Maler. It seemed to troll that Maler should mind his own business. The problem was that Maler — unlike his parents — worshipped an entity called G (who had created troll). G was not thrilled with people living on the sidewalk and let it be known that troll was to have a home like everyone else.

So you know what Maler did? Maler got all of those who worshipped G and together with troll they talked about what to do. It would be great to say that troll was happy about what was going on but the truth of the matter was that he was very suspicious. Troll was very fearful of the opinion of those who heard him sing. He was very dependent on them for the handouts they provided him. Maler had a home. Maler did not have to concern himself with shelter or food.

It was many years later when troll could no longer sing that he was to thank Maler. He told Maler that at the time he thought Maler was trying to replace him with another troll. He explained to Maler that it was not that he liked living on the sidewalk, but rather his fear of losing his spot on the sidewalk caused him to resist being placed. People knew him and in exchange for his singing gave him the money he required to eat. He did not want to lose the little that he had. He was dependent on being accessible to them and that spot ensured this.

Troll never got around to worshipping G, but this did not matter. G was happy troll was no longer living on the sidewalk, and Maler was glad that G was happy. And my dear ones, that is the once upon a time story about Maler and the troll.

The Eagle Cried

Sitting beside Helen's bed, I heard the eagle cry. Helen's chest heaved up and quickly fell down. I knew it was not a matter of months but rather days.

Hours sometimes chain together in a dosey doe rhythm of forward movement.

The geese knew this. When the time comes they form a V-shaped formation in the sky.

I thought it would be soon. I saw her mouth hang open as if it was grasping for air. I hoped for Helen that the geese would come soon and take her spirit to the spirit world. She sighed. She sensed my presence. Her eyes opened and I sensed her bewilderment. She must have wondered where the needles in her arms came from. Her eyes looked at me. There was a recognition. Her feet moved and as if blinds held on a cord, her eyelids pulled down and she returned to sleep. Chest ascending then descending. I wondered if she heard the eagle cry.

Walking out of the hospital I saw the geese. We nodded at each other in acknowledgement. They returned to pacing; the flight was not to occur then. I left them and took the subway home. When I exited the subway I looked to the sky and there was nothing.

A few days later, I heard them before I saw them. They honked as they flew in a perfect V-formation in the sky. My heart felt relief and pain all at the same time. The phone rang. I did not bother to answer it. I simply opened the door to my home, put on the kettle, and sat in the quietness of the room. Then I pressed the re-call button on the phone.

She Led

Life is a black canvas with streaks of yellow
Something like a dark womb
A quiet formation
A silent emersion
Full of mini contractions

How is it possible that she led
What did I miss
Maybe nothing

What could have possibly provoked the huge water burst
The tightness of the channel
The severity of the contractions
The yellow streaks
Pulsating around me

How is it possible that she led
What did I miss
Maybe nothing

Of course the arrival is never anything like they talk about
It always seems cold, foreboding
Thank God for the yellow streaks
The distance from the womb
The inner knowing

How is it possible that she led
What did I miss
Maybe nothing

Another contraction
Thank God for the yellow streaks
Which cut light into the darkness
That provide the evidence of sustainability
The formation of creativity

She led
I missed nothing
She led

Life is a black canvas with streaks of yellow
Something like a dark womb
A quiet formation
A silent emersion
Full of mini contractions

Who Is the Host?

Creation exists and takes its energy from many sources. It is said that it needs transference not only to coexist but to regenerate itself. I say rubbish. Domination and control, that is what creation needs.

It is said that the leaves participate — like a human — in an exchange. It — like a human — sweats. Okay, so the word is transpiration but my point is that there is nothing of this coexistence, cooperative crap. What is really going on is the establishment of feeding rights.

Sit down and I will tell you a story. It is a story of a relationship between a tree and a human.

As you know the life of a human — compared to a tree — can be quite short. For example there are no human beings that I know of who live two hundred years or more but there are plenty of trees in the world that share the aforementioned age. The question is how do they survive so long? I believe I have the perfect story to answer that question. Before I start I need to tell you a few things.

I was raised by demons, excuse me I meant to say parents. I was brought up by parents who experimented on those of the lower intelligence. The reason they never sought those with a higher intellect was because of the inflammatory effect those that the higher intellect had on their bodies. Unfortunately I have inherited this tendency. These days the matter is especially complicated.

It is complicated by education. Education is starting to become universal and the negative side effect to this is people are tending to question more these days. I mean there used to be volumes of people who would faint or freeze. Now everyone wants to discuss and critically analyze. It really is quite unsettling.

We demons are dependent on the compliance (regardless of the reason) of those we feed from. There can be no intellectual debate. Submission. There has to be submission.

Those of us who have the inflammatory response are left in the terrible position of having to convince people of what we are entitled to, our feed! It is ridiculous!!

The last one before you I did not take the time to convince and the inflammation I experienced — because of this person's lack of submission — was beyond any point of tolerance. My stomach extended to twice its size and I got a terrible pain in my stomach. Oh, I shudder just at the thought of the ordeal I was subjected to. I have decided that I simply will not go through that ordeal again. The question of who is the host needs to be clearly established once and for all so that our feed can be without inflammation. There has to be compliance, some level of willingness, or at the very least an appreciation of the order of things.

A host has — as far as I am concerned — a right to be fed. It is entitled to be fed.

Dominance, order, and control, these are the qualities necessary. The story I am going to tell you and the newspaper clipping you will read after the story should provide you some understanding and enable you to submit. The story is about a conversation a human has with a tree over several decades and may I say it is also about feeding rights. I will now play the tape.

"Hello, it is so nice to be with you again. The winter was so cold and I was far too busy to rest in your branches. I thought of you often though. I see your children are starting to grow. They have blossomed so beautiful.

Per the agreement you had with my mother, I kept all the seeds and they are ready for planting."

"Yes, I made the usual apple pies and sauces but this year your children also participated in being smoothies."

"Quite right, I did not know what a smoothie was until my niece from Toronto came down. She told me that smoothies are like applesauce that you drink."

"So glad you approve of your children becoming smoothies. I did think to make the trip and ask you but it was so cold. Since you already agreed for your children to participate in becoming applesauce and pies I thought you would not mind them also being smoothies. So glad you are pleased."

"Yes, I kept all the children together. I kept the agreement. Not one of your children participated alone.

Back to the seeds; did you have a specific place this year where you would like to see them planted?"

"Okay, I'll wait. I can see you are very busy this year."

"Thank you for asking. My legs are a bit stiff. With Mark being sick I did not get out walking much. Maybe I will climb up unto your branches next week. You can tell me where you want the seeds planted then.

On another totally different topic do you realize that we have been together seventy years now?"

"How long were you with my mother?"

"Yes, I thought it was for eighty years.

Just here at the base of your trunk was where she used to breast feed me. She told all the stories about how she planted you and all the fun you two had. You were always there for her. Even on her death bed she felt you. No one knew how she got the strength to actually die in your branches. Glad I found her; had a feeling she would be here. What fun times we had. I remembered the blossoms on you when she died. They were magnificent.

I see that the branch Dad hung a swing on for me is still there.

Thought the branch might break during that ice storm we had this winter.

Until next week then. Nice big hug."

"Oh that felt good. Anyone seeing me hug you would think I'm a bit off.

Who hugs a tree these days?

By the way they never did find out about you and Mom. Even Dad did not know about you two. Such fun memories we had."

"Funny you should know. I don't remember telling you. Yes, I am expecting a grandchild soon. See you next week."

"Hello, again. Did I tell you about the National Geographic film about the turtles on the coast of Trinidad?"

"No, well I'll tell you. You are not alone. Some of turtles have been laying eggs for as long as you have been birthing blossoms. Seems us humans are the short-lived ones. I wonder if you'll be around when my grandchild is my age of seventy. Wouldn't that be wonderful!

Did a lot of walking and stretching this week so I can walk up the ladder Dad built on you.

Mark finally got put in a nursing home.

Oh, I love this view.

I won't miss all of his nastiness but I do find I miss his company as he used to be before he got sick.

I can almost feel Mom here as I sit on your branches. Where do you want the seeds to be planted?"

"Hmmm didn't think of that place. Good idea. One more look before I leave and of course a big hug."

"Hello, I'm back. Oh look at your children. They are so beautiful. I do not think I have ever seen your children so healthy looking. So many of them."

"Will gladly let them participate in becoming the filling in the apple pie, the sauce in the applesauce, and the smoothie.

Been doing quite a bit of walking now that Mark is in the locked ward. Turns out he has got some brain tumour that they cannot operate on.

What a view. So beautiful. I see so much from your branches.

Our daughter has a child now. I was wondering if it would be alright to bring her up here to see the view."

"Wonderful. Will bring her up soon. Told my daughter about you but she just looked at me strange. Mom told me that sometimes these knowings skip a generation. So it is okay. Big hug and see you soon."

"Well that didn't work out. Sorry about that. Lord, that child is hateful."

"Been a few years now. I see you have no blossoms."

"Me, I'm heading to 85 and slowing down quite a bit. That grandchild was a handful. How about you? How are you doing?"

"Yes, it seems that old age has got the best of us."

"Just felt I just needed to see you today.

Got this pain down my arm and I just wanted to rest where Mom use to breast feed me.

I also want to tell you I really enjoyed all these conversations over the years. You know, like Mom, you helped me a lot even though I wasn't with you. Just knowing you're here was so helpful. So reliable, you were the only one that was so reliable."

"Think I'll take a nap before I go back. It is so beautiful here.

Thank you."

So now that you have heard the human, read the newspaper article.

Newspaper article: "Old woman found dead; her body was found sitting upright, resting against a tree. No one knows how the branches got wrapped around her body. When an attempt to move her body occurred a branch holding a swing fell down from the tree killing the ambulance driver. Members from the emergency task force started to hack at the branches with their axes. After the first cut, huge gobs of sap started coating the axes making them useless. The ground started to shake and suddenly the earth around the tree started opening up. All ran away.

When they returned the next day, the old lady was nowhere to be found. The tree was full of blossoms."

So you heard the human and have read the newspaper article, now tell me, who is the host? The tree, which is still alive, or that dead old woman. Were the seeds planted in the human body, planted in the soil only to regenerate later?

Who is the host? Ah, I see your doubt. You need to trust me, it is the order of things. No one is to blame. Now be quiet and compliant. It is time for the feeder to be fed. It will not hurt a bit.

Remember

I remember you watching with longing as she walked up the aisle. I remember you watching with fury when she said "I Do" in the ceremony. At the time, I was quite sure that the tears falling down her face were not from joy. I was absolutely sure.

I want you to know that I have called her and she is coming. I see your longing for her even though you are dying in the hospice. I see your desire to be with her, even though we have been together twenty-eight years.

There is something I want to tell you before she arrives. What I want to tell you is that I have loved you for over thirty years. I love you now and I will love you until the end of time.

Ahh, there she is. Before I close the door and give both of you privacy, remember I love you. For if you do not remember, where will our together memories exist?

In the Wound, Wounding

I felt him when he was in the wound. The dark bluish murky substance oozed down the outline of his body. It stopped and gelled. I was not clear where it came from.

Without moving his head, his vacant eyes stared at the white walls. Sitting in the wound, he picked at the scab. The ooze contained in the gel seeped out. A sigh escaped from his lips.

He smiled at his family when they returned for a visit. It was a polite smile which revealed nothing. Knowing that they would bankrupt him if he released the money, he pretended not be present during the discussion of funding arrangements. Several times they came only to leave in fury.

He was very aware that he taught them that the weak craft their vulnerability. Disease, he taught them, was self-willed; otherwise, he had told them, it would not exist. Now — after a great deal of expenditure and unsuccessful traditional as well as mainstream treatments — he was still ill.

He deeply regretted what he had taught them, not because of any moral reason but rather self-preservation. You see as far as they were concerned his vulnerability meant he was a target, fair game. The hunter was the hunted. He found the demotion humiliating.

When he first arrived he tried to inform the staff that he was now the one being hunted. He tried to tell them how humiliating it was. The staff patted his hand while smiling sweetly and informed the doctor of his delusions.

Medication was prescribed. It fogged his mind to such a point that he truly did not know where he was. Deciding it was time to play patient, he thanked them for the medication and reported to them that members of his family were not trying to kill him. He told them that he must have had a breakdown.

He then started to insist that he obtain more medication. The more he insisted on having medication, the more the medical staff united in their belief that he was drug seeking. Quite quickly he was taken off all mood-altering medication. He pretended to be upset but in truth was quite happy. Now his mind was clear. Of course various family members were infuriated. The removal of the medication occurred during the time when they finally were able to obtain a capsule which — over a period of time — would have killed him without any trace.

"Think of it as a time released death vitamin," said the dealer.

I sighed. He looked at me. I took the mop and continued to wash the floor. In those days I was really good at cleaning the floors and emptying out the garbage cans. Usually I only talked to the dying. I cannot say why I spoke to him that day but I did.

"Compassion cannot be taught," I said.

"No, it has to be felt," he said.

"And you," I asked, "do you feel the compassion?"

"It's in me now. Came after I could not fix the wound," he said.

"I figured it was in you. Saw how you looked at Hillary," I said.

"Yes, she's got it bad." He lifted his head to look at me. "Really bad. Don't know how she tolerates all that pain. God, that chemo is terrible."

I decided it was time to leave and moved towards the door. He asked my name. I looked at him and wondered what the interest was.

"What's your interest in the likes of me?" I asked.

"Well," he said, "I see you around. You always seem to be cleaning up."

"It's what I do well," I said.

He stared into me. "I saw you pray with Hillary the other day," he said.

"It was on my break," I said cautiously.

"No, no, no, I'm not going to report you! Just wondering if you would do the same for me?" he asked.

"No, I won't do that," I said. "You're not of my faith. You should speak to the Chaplain about that."

"Then I will," he said.

"I'll tell you something though," I said.

"What?" he asked.

"My grandmother told me that in WWI her father flew a plane that ended up in the sea. She said that her father's wounds did not kill him because of the sea water. Maybe since you are oozing you should wash yourself in the sea."

He looked at me in amazement. The next day I was told to clean his room up. He had left. His family was in a rage.

About a year later I was emptying the garbage and who should I see in a wheelchair but him. He smiled.

"The sea water and the medication helped," he said. "I just wanted to thank you and your Grandmother."

I looked at him. I did not see anything oozing along his body. He looked a bit frail but that was about it.

"Are you praying?" I asked. Before he answered me, his phone rang and he answered it. He then started yelling and cursing at the caller.

No, he was not praying. He was hunting. Definitely. I could hear it in the tone of his voice. I left him, in the wound, wounding. Turned out he yelled so much that he had a heart attack. Right there in the hallway. Being in the wound, wounding has its consequences.

Priya

He loved her; his heart leaped over itself with joy at the sight of her. When he gave her the fish, her finger touched his, and it was as though an electric current struck his heart. Being unable to speak to her. He had to make arrangements to see her, and this took a long time.

Four months had passed before he made the connection. Interestingly enough, the connection was with the sixth cousin removed. She — the sixth cousin — worked with his beloved's father. Introductions were made, and the appointment scheduled. A total of five months to meet her.

She loved him; her heart leaped over itself with joy at the sight of him. When he gave her the fish, her finger touched his, and it was as though an electric current struck her heart. Being unable to speak to him, she had to make arrangements to see him without anyone's knowledge, and this took a long time.

Four months had passed before she made the connection. Interestingly enough the connection was her father's accountant.

She noticed her beloved speaking to her father's accountant at the market. The following day she went to her father's office and arranged — quite slyly I may add — a meeting with her father's accountant. It was then she found out that he was also interested in her.

They sat opposite to each other, and both were overjoyed. It was during the second meeting that the doubt entered. The parents had gone into a separate room, leaving them together. She looked at him, and his eyes quickly darted away. Feeling as if a knife had sliced her heart open, she barely was able to catch her breath. Doubt — not about his love — entered her.

During the second meeting, the parents went into a separate room leaving them together. This opportunity of being alone with her excited him so much that he could feel a part of his body raising and starting to stretch the piece of clothing he had covering it. Terror struck his heart. It was at this point that he looked away from her. He knew what she felt. He felt what she felt but said nothing. He knew of her doubt.

Ten great-grandchildren later, he lay in bed dying. Their age spotted fingers intertwined. She kissed his forehead, and in doing so, her gray hair fell upon his white hair.

She took in a very deep breath and asked him why he looked away that day. Smilingly, he gestured her to put her ear to his mouth. She did, and he told her, pointing down to that part of his body, which right until his sickness so easily stretched at the sight of her. Her laughter filled the room, and the faint scar on her heart evaporated. He felt it immediately.

When his life went into the other life, she continued to laugh. She watched her children and grandchildren in the market selling the fish. The smell of the market, the thickness of the night air; all were part of him, so she never felt alone. There was, of course, the fact that their love was untouched by death. She was determined not to doubt him again. Truth be known, when they met again, she never did, and as for him, he included her in his most private thoughts.

Email your top three favorite stories
to   boucaudinthestory7@gmail.com

www.boucaudinthestory2013-2017.com

CPSIA information can be obtained
at www.ICGtesting.com
Printed in the USA
LVOW11s0347011217
558251LV00001B/48/P